To Kyle,
        Reach for the stars!

THE
TELESCOPE
TRAVELERS

Peter A. Oppenheim

For Sarah and Kyle

The Telescope Travelers

Special thanks to NASA and STScI for their amazing photographs,
and to Susan for –everything else.

ISBN 978-1-4303-0795-2
Published By Lulu
For Garden Spot Press

Visit us at www.thetelescopetravelers.com

TABLE OF CONTENTS

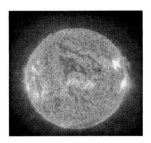

Chapter One
Like Sand on the Beach

The sky was like black velvet. The stars were tiny diamonds sprinkled everywhere she looked. As 11-year-old Taylor and her younger brother Zack walked along the beach, she tried to count them, "25, 26, 27, 28," Taylor said. "16, 58, 97, 32," Zack called out. "Stop it, you're messing up my count," Taylor complained. Zack just giggled and said, "You'll never count them all, there are too many," and he went back to looking down at the sand. Zack, it seemed, was more interested in the water as it washed up on the shore, stopping about a foot away from them before it was pulled back toward the vast ocean. "There must be millions of stars, no, billions. I bet there are more stars than grains of sand on this beach," said Taylor. "Wow!" she whispered.

Taylor had never seen so dark a sky and so many stars before. From their backyard about an hour away from the city, she had seen stars before, but the light pollution had always kept the sky a light gray. The brightness of her backyard sky had washed out the view leaving only the brightest stars visible. "There," she said pointing north, "that's the big dipper. I remember it from my Girl Scout camping trip, see?" Zack looked up, searching.

"AHHHH!!" Zack's scream cut through the sound of the surf hitting the shoreline. "What is it? What is it!?" Taylor yelled, but Zack was running. She took off after him, struggling to get her footing in the sand. She knew she could run faster than this, but with every step she took, she felt her feet sink into the soft sand. Zack finally stopped running 30 feet ahead of her. Taylor caught up to him, but it took her a while longer to catch her breath. "What…is…wrong?" she panted. "The wave, it got my sneakers wet! That water's cold!!" he said. "That's it?" Taylor said in disgust. "That's why you ran off screaming? Ugggggh," she groaned. "Brothers!"

The next morning came quickly. There was something about the sea air that helped them sleep. Maybe it was the cool breeze that blew through the window screens on their family's rented beach house, or perhaps it was the sound of the waves rolling in and out over and over again. "Breakfast!" came the call from their mother. She had set out four bowls of cereal and a plate with orange wedges.

Zack was first to the table, grabbing the largest piece of orange as he sat. "What are we doing today?" Taylor asked as she entered, yawning. She shuffled to the table rubbing her eyes and chose the seat across from her brother. "Since it's our last day on vacation, I thought we'd spend it relaxing on the beach," her father said as he walked up behind her. He was already wearing his bathing suit. It was the one that looked like a painter had splattered a whole palette's worth of brightly colored paint on it. "That's a great idea," her mother said. "I'll pack a picnic lunch and we can spend the day." "Do I have to go in the water?" Zack asked. "Not if you don't want to," his mother replied, "but I really wish you would get over this fear of yours. You can't avoid water forever. Now come here and let me put some sunscreen on you."

After the table was cleared and the kids had placed the dishes in the sink, they gathered their hats, towels and a big bag full of beach toys. Zack slipped his feet into his sneakers only to hear a squoosh sound. "Oh no," he said, "they aren't dry yet!" Squish squoosh squish squoosh was the only sound they heard as they walked down the path toward the beach.

Chapter Two

"X" Marks the Spot

The kids didn't have to walk far down the sidewalk to find the place where the concrete ended and the sand began. For Zack it couldn't come soon enough. He wanted those cold, wet sneakers off. With every step he had taken, he was reminded of his fight with the ocean wave the night before. Come to think of it, it wasn't much of a fight. The wave came in, soaked his sneakers and he ran away, screaming. It was a bit embarrassing and he tried to tell himself that he'd be stronger next time. After all, he was 8 years old!

Taylor was just as excited to take off her flip-flops and walk barefoot in the sand. It was warm and soft and felt good between her toes as the ocean came into view over the top of a sand dune. They walked with their heads down this time. It was a clean beach, since people were good about taking their trash with them when they left, but there was still plenty to see, or step on. Bits of driftwood were scattered around and looked like miniature trees that had been worn smooth from the power of the salt water.

"Here's a good one!" Taylor called as she bent down to pick up a creamy white colored shell. It had ridges running across its top and a tiny hole at one end. "I'm going to make a necklace out of this one. I'll put a string through this hole and hang it around my neck. It will be beautiful," she said proudly.

"Look what I found," Zack called from a few steps away. He ran up to Taylor holding something green, slimy and shiny. It was dangling from the tips of his fingers as though he wasn't sure he really wanted to hold it. He held it up to within 3 inches of Taylor's face and she automatically pulled her head back. "Seaweed," she said. "It must have washed up on the shore when the tide came in." "But where did it come from?" Zack asked. "From the ocean," Taylor replied. "It's a sea plant that grows under the water." "Really? You mean it was alive?" "Sure, the ocean is filled with living things, fish, plants, lots of animals of all shapes and sizes," she explained. "Mr. Capella, my science teacher, says the ocean is where the first life on Earth formed." "Cool," Zack answered, and ran off to find more.

"Kids?" their father called. "We'll set up here, give me a hand." Zack and Taylor ran back and together they spread out the blanket and put shoes in each corner to help hold it down. Then they put their pails and shovels and bags of food at one end of the blanket and their parents' books at the other. Their father stuck a large umbrella into the sand, shading their spot for the day.

"Let's dig for buried treasure!" Zack announced. "Where should we dig, Dad?" "Hmm," he said, "let's see, how about...here," he declared, making an "X" in the sand with his heal. "OK," Zack agreed, "X marks the spot," and he grabbed his shovel. "I bet I can dig all the way to the other side of the Earth!" he said as he began burrowing into the ground. Taylor doubted this, but decided to join in anyway and picked up the other shovel. They dug and dug. As the hole got deeper, the pile of sand next to them got higher and higher. "Look Dad," Zack called, "we're building up at the same time we're digging down!" "That's nice," said his father without looking up from his book.

The Sun was nearly straight overhead by now and the hole was deep enough for Taylor to lie down in. Zack suggested she climb in, hoping that he'd get the chance to cover his sister with sand, but Taylor had a better idea. "Let's bury Dad in the sand!" she suggested. "Yeah," Zack excitedly replied. "Come on Dad, can we? Please?" "Well OK," he answered, "but you'll have to dig a deeper hole than that. I won't fit." "Yes!" the kids hissed at the same time. Both pushed their shovels into the ground with new energy. The sound of the shovels cutting through the cool damp sand got louder and faster. They dug for another 20 minutes until Zack pushed his shovel in for what seemed like the thousandth time. Only this time, the sound he heard was not the shush of plastic through sand. No, this sound was a definite "snap." "Uh oh," Zack said as he pulled only the handle part of his shovel out of the sand. "My shovel broke!" he moaned. "Oh no," Taylor said sadly, "I guess you must have hit a rock or something." "Or something," Zack replied as he reached into the hole and pulled out a handful of sand. A small patch of something smooth could now be seen at the bottom of the hole. "This looks flat, I wonder how big it is," he said.

Their father lay on the blanket nearby so focused on his book he hadn't noticed the new development. Their mother had turned away so the sun wouldn't hit her face. Her eyes were closed and as far as they could tell she was probably asleep.

Taylor was still digging at her end. They had cleared a hole a foot and a half deep already. Zack was using both hands now, pulling out handfuls of sand in an effort to find the edges of whatever this thing was. He tapped it with his knuckles. BONK BONK BONK was the hollow sounding noise it made. "Hey Taylor, I think this thing is metal, some kind of box." Taylor stopped her own digging and looked up at Zack. They both looked down at the hole. They looked up at each other. They looked back at the hole. They looked up at each other and at the same time screamed, "treasure chest!" At that, they both dove into the hole and began throwing sand out of it like two big dogs in a race to find their favorite bone.

Sand was flying everywhere, including their own blanket. This wouldn't have been much of a problem except for the fact that their parents were *on* the blanket. "Hey! Hey! Hey! What are you kids doing! Stop throwing sand!" their father warned. Their mother must have been asleep because she didn't even move. The kids suddenly became still. "Um, oh, sorry Dad." "Yeah, sorry Dad," they both replied as he went back to his book. The kids looked at each other, smiled a guilty smile, shrugged their shoulders and went back to digging.

They quickly found the edges of the box and reached in to pull it from the sand.

Chapter Three

Treasure!

Taylor got her fingers under one end and Zack the other. It was heavy, but not so much that they couldn't handle it. Together they lifted the long gray case out of the hole and set it down next to the large mound of sand they had created. They dusted it off and inspected it. It was about three feet long and ten inches wide. It was made of a dull gray metal and was in perfect condition.

"It's not exactly what I expected a treasure chest to look like," said Taylor. "What did you expect?" asked Zack. "You know," she said shrugging her shoulders, "big and wooden with a rounded top and big handles, and all beat up like it's been buried forever. This one looks brand new." She continued, "It looks as though it was just buried here, no rust, no scratches, dents, handles or..." she paused, "latches," Taylor said with a confused sound in her voice. "You're right," Zack said. "How are we supposed to open this thing?" he wondered aloud. "Let's turn it over and see if there's anything on the other side," he suggested. As they did, they were surprised to see the only marks anywhere on the box. Three symbols were displayed along one side of their find.

"BINGO!" said Zack. "How does this help us open it?" Taylor asked. "No clue, but we're making progress," he said with a hopeful smile. They brushed the remaining grains of sand from the three symbols and examined them more closely. Each was about 2 inches big and was a part of the metal the way George Washington's head is part of a quarter. Taylor gently ran her fingers across them, feeling the difference in texture from the smooth side of the box.

The first symbol was made of three simple lines. Two of the lines started from a point. One went up to the right and the other down to the right. The third line was curved and connected the upper and lower lines.

The second symbol consisted of two parallel lines with an oval connecting them at one end and a curved line at the other. A smaller version of itself sat on top.

The third symbol, a circle with spikes, looked like this:

One symbol was in each of the top two corners. The third was centered at the bottom of the box side. The symbols sat there silently commanding the kids to decipher them. What did they mean? Were they a lock to open the mysteries of the box, or just strange decorations? Maybe they were instructions of some kind, or the family crest of the owner. In any case, they didn't look like any pirate symbols they had ever seen.

"Maybe they're buttons," Zack said as he began pushing on each of the strange markings in order. He touched the first, nothing happened. He touched the second, no response. He touched the third and as he did, they heard a low rumbling, stuttering sound that grew in volume until it was louder than the ocean waves crashing on the beach and louder than the sound of the vacationers nearby laughing and playing. "QuooooOOOOCH!" Zack and Taylor jumped backwards, landing next to their blanket near their father's head. The sound began again, growing in intensity just as the fear was growing in Taylor and Zack. "QuooooOOOOCH!" All at once, they realized the sound was actually coming from behind them and they turned and looked to identify the source. There, face down in his book, was their father snoring away and totally unaware of the kid's big find. They smiled at each other in a way that said, "I knew it was Dad all the time and I wasn't scared for a minute and I won't say anything if you don't." They returned to the box.

"There's something familiar about this first symbol," Taylor said, "I just know it." "This last one looks like light to me; see how the light rays come out of it?" Zack offered. "Yeah, I see what you mean, but the light is coming from all around it. I think it looks more like the Sun or a star," Taylor explained. "Well, it doesn't have points like a star…" Zack wondered aloud. "Silly, the Sun *is* a star and they don't actually have points. Mr. Capella taught us that real stars are burning balls of gas. Our Sun is just an average star," she announced. "Oh, OK, I can see that," he said.

"That's it!" Taylor screamed. "That's the first symbol!" "What is?" Zack asked, his head tilted and a confused look on his face once again. "*I can see that*, that's what you said," Taylor repeated. "Yeah, so?" Zack said slowly. "Don't you see?" she pleaded. "What, what?" Zack asked with annoyance growing in his voice. "It's an eye, you know, that you see with, a side view of one!" she blurted out. "Oh, why didn't you say so, I *can* see that," he replied, finally understanding.

Now they both looked down at the middle symbol, staring at it with such intensity that if their eyes were lasers they could burn right through the mysterious metal case. They were close to solving the mystery and they both knew it. They silently puzzled over the equation. *An eye plus something equals a star*, each thought. *An eye plus something that looks like tubes equals a star*, their minds repeated. A moment passed and then at the same time they looked up at each other, and as if only one of them was speaking the answer came from their lips: "Telescope!"

"Huh, what?" mumbled their father as he took a deep breath and turned over on his back, his eyes still closed. "Oh, uh, nothing Dad, go back to sleep," Taylor replied. "OK honey, I'll take out the trash later," was the mumbled response as he drifted off again. They both watched to be sure he was asleep again and when the snoring resumed, they knew it was safe to continue.

"Let's open it," Zack said eagerly. "But how?" Taylor asked. "We understand the symbols, but that doesn't tell us how to open it." "I think it does," Zack confidently replied. "Watch," he said. He put his left thumb on the eye symbol, then he placed his right thumb on the telescope symbol. "It's an equation, you know, like math. Now you put your thumb on the star symbol," he told her. She reached out with her hand and slowly, gently rested her thumb on the star symbol. Almost immediately, the side of the box popped up under their fingers and a puff of air sprayed out of the box as if it had been waiting a long time to escape. They both flinched in surprise as though someone had sneaked up behind them and tapped them on the back.

They looked at each other with a mixture of shock and surprise that quickly turned to pride at their success. After a quick glance around to be sure no one was watching, Taylor lifted the lid all the way up, revealing the mystery hidden inside their treasure chest. What they saw was shiny and silver, but it wasn't pirate coins. It was two of the shiniest metal tubes they had ever seen. One was long, about as long as Taylor's arm, and had a diameter of about 4 inches at one end. The other end was much smaller. The second tube was only 8 inches long with a diameter of only an inch at both ends. They ran their hands across the metal and felt its cool smooth surface.

"It *is* a telescope," whispered Taylor. "Looks like two telescopes to me," Zack added. "The little one is called the finder scope. It helps you point the bigger one. I wonder where it came from," she said. "Finders keepers, losers weepers," sang Zack. "It's our's now," he announced. "Well, only until we find the true owner," Taylor cautioned. It was at that moment that Taylor realized it had somehow gotten quieter. The snoring had stopped and it was a relief to have only the normal sounds of the beach back. But if the snoring had stopped, they realized, it could mean only one thing, their father was waking up.

Chapter Four

First Light

A s their mini-van pulled into the driveway, Taylor and Zack's parents sighed at the realization that their vacation was over and their regular routine would soon begin again. In fact, they were so focused on being home and the immediate need for food shopping, lawn mowing and laundry to be done, that they didn't even realize how unusually helpful the kids were being in unloading the van. So much so that they never noticed the extra item wrapped up in a large beach towel that the kids had had since they left the beach. Luckily, the kids had been able to cover their buried treasure before anyone had seen it and simply bundled it with the rest of their things when their parents awoke earlier on the beach. They had agreed to hide it under Taylor's bed since the space under Zack's was already filled with, well, not even Zack was sure what was under there and they decided that now was not the time to find out.

The following day the kids, anxious to try out the telescope, left the house following breakfast. Earlier, the two had been delighted to find how perfectly the box fit inside Zack's baseball equipment bag. With the bats, balls and glove carefully stored in his closet, Zack carried the bag over his shoulder to the park near their house. They had the park to themselves and they unpacked the bag at home plate. At the bottom of the silver container they found the tripod to hold the telescope and another small box containing two screws, one green and one red. "How does it work?" Zack asked. Taylor recalled her astronomy unit in school and demonstrated how to spread the three legs of the tripod and attach the larger telescope to it. Then she snapped the finder on top of the larger tube.

"Let me see, let me see," Zack begged, nudging Taylor to the side. He looked into the finder with his right eye and closed his left. Zack saw two thin lines that crossed exactly at the center of the view. He knew they were there to help aim the telescope. He was looking at the swing set at the opposite side of the park. It looked large and very close. "Cool," he said. He pulled his head back to look without the finder. He could barely see the swing set, it was just a small spot in the distance.

He moved his eye back to the finder and noticed the lines crossing on the seat of the swing next to the slide. Next he moved his eye to the eyepiece of the larger, main telescope. "Ah," he groaned, "I don't think it's working. I can't see anything, it's all black." "Really?" Taylor asked, "let me have a look." Zack stepped aside and Taylor put her eye to the large scope. She gently twisted the focus knob to sharpen the view. "Hmm," she said, "Let's see what you're aimed at." She moved her eye to the finder and said, "It's working alright, wow that's powerful!" She turned to Zack and said, "You're seeing that swing so close up the seat fills the whole view." "No way," he replied in disbelief as he stepped up to look again. "Cool!" he declared. "Astronomers call this 'first light', the first time a new telescope is used," Taylor lectured. "Let me guess," Zack mocked, "Mr. Capella told you that."

"What are these screws? I wonder where they go?" Taylor asked out loud. "They're probably extras," Zack answered, "Dad always says he has extra screws after he puts something together. I wouldn't worry about it." Taylor looked around the telescope in an effort to find a place for the screws. "Hey, let's look at the Sun, I bet we can see fire burning." "No, don't!" Taylor interrupted. "Mr. Capella told us never to look at the Sun directly or without special equipment. He told us it's so strong it could permanently damage our eyes." "Oh yeah? Well I thought you said the Sun was a star and we can look at stars,

18

can't we?" Zack challenged. "Yes, because those other stars are so much farther away they can't hurt us," she explained. "OK, is that why I don't need sunscreen when I go out at night?" he asked. "Something like that," she answered.

"Here's a spot," Taylor announced upon noticing a hole on the side of the finder. "Maybe one of the screws goes in here." She picked up the green screw and turned it in the hole. Then she leaned over for a look. As she put her eye to the eyepiece of the telescope she began to feel strange, a bit dizzy. Suddenly it seemed to be getting darker and she felt as if she was starting to float in mid air. She tried to call Zack's name, but no sound came out. As Zack watched, he couldn't believe his eyes. Taylor's whole body was starting to twist into a spiral like an upside down tornado. She was spinning faster and faster. He stood there watching and unsure of what to do. He screamed her name and as he did, the spinning funnel cloud that only seconds before was his sister was sucked into the eyepiece like water down a drain! Zack fell backwards stunned. The whole thing had only taken a couple of seconds. She had vanished. He was left alone, sitting in the dirt with the telescope.

The sky was clear and the wind calm. It was a beautiful day. Zack picked himself up and looked around. Where had she gone? Did she actually get sucked into the telescope? Was that possible? What was going on and what had he just seen. Zack decided to look into the scope and see if she was in there. He carefully, nervously stepped up to the eyepiece and looked. It was still a dark view, but there was some movement, though he couldn't tell what he was looking at. He moved his eye to the finder for a wider view. What he saw startled him so much he stumbled back, falling once again to the dirt. "It couldn't be," he whispered aloud.

Chapter Five

Directions

Taylor's eyes were squeezed tightly shut and her feet were off the ground. She was swaying slightly and her hands had a tight grip on some cold, uneven metal that was now on both sides of her. It was mostly quiet except for the sense that a distant voice was calling her name. She tried to calm herself and realized that she was sitting. "Sitting, yet moving, with my feet off the ground? But I was…" she wondered to herself. Slowly she opened one eye and then the other. Both eyes looked to the right and then to the left, then back again. They shifted back and forth several times before she finally let out the breath she hadn't realized she was holding. She was sitting on one of the swings, holding the chains and looking across the park toward the baseball diamond. There in the distance she saw the source of the voice calling her name. It was Zack. He was jumping up and down and wildly waving his arms. He had just begun to run toward her.

Taylor released her grip on the chains and allowed herself to slide off the swing. She felt strangely reassured, then excited, when her feet made solid contact with the ground. She took off in a run across the field and they met half way. Both of them, totally out of breath, began speaking immediately, neither aware nor caring that the other was also speaking. Their words became jumbled together. "Did you see... are you... what was... how did you... oh my... so cool... let me try!!" Then Zack got a full sentence out. "How did you do that?" he asked eagerly. "I, I don't know. I just looked into the eyepiece and the next thing I knew I felt light-headed. I seem to remember flying through some kind of tunnel. Then I found myself sitting on the swing," Taylor replied. "That's where the telescope was aimed," Zack added. "But I looked in it too, how come it didn't send me?" "I don't know, maybe only one person can travel at a time," she theorized. "Well, think, what did you do just before you looked into it?" he questioned. "Nothing special," she said, "I just adjusted the focus knob." "Yeah, well there must be something else," he said, "think." "The screw, the green screw," she recalled. "I inserted the green screw into the finder just before my last look. That must be how we turn it on. Come on, let's go."

As they ran back to the spot where they had left the telescope, Taylor told Zack, "You know, it's a good thing it was only pointed across the park. What if it had been aimed at someplace farther away? How would I have gotten back?"

As they approached home plate, they went right for the finder. "Wait a minute," Zack interrupted, "that wasn't here before." Taylor saw what Zack meant. "You're right" she agreed, "at least I didn't notice it." Next to the green screw, a small screen had appeared on the side of the finder tube. Words on the screen read:

Ready. Earth. Hold finder. Red to Return.

Taylor removed the screw. The words faded and then the screen seemed to soften and dissolve into the metal. A moment later, the surface was smooth and solid and there was no sign of the screen ever having been there. "Awesome, did you see that!" Zack yelled. "Now put it back," he said. She did, and the side of the finder appeared to turn to liquid for a moment, the metal rippling like a silver wave, and then hardened in the shape of the screen. The words faded back into view.

Ready. Earth. Hold finder. Red to Return.

"Well, I guess we have our answer," Taylor declared.

She removed the screw again and the screen vanished into the metal once more. "It's my turn now, I want to try," Zack demanded. "OK, I guess," she allowed, "but take the red screw with you this time." Zack put the red screw in his pocket. "Let's try that bench down there," he said, holding one hand up to his forehead to shield the Sun and pointing with the other. He turned the telescope on the tripod in the direction of the bench and looked into the finder. Then he adjusted the position very slightly to put the crosshairs exactly on the spot. "OK," he said, exhaling heavily. "Here I go." Taylor handed him the green screw and he gently inserted it into the hole on the side of the finder, giggling nervously as he did it. The silver panel liquified and formed the screen and words they had just seen a moment ago. He reached up and placed his hand on the finder. "Count down 5, 4, 3, 2, 1 blast off!" Zack called as he put his eye to the eyepiece.

Just as before, a spinning funnel cloud that was larger at its bottom than its top quickly formed where Zack had stood. Then, the top of the cloud tipped over and was sucked into the gleaming silver tube. Zack found himself flying through a beautiful tunnel that curved up and down and occasionally from side to side. It was dark, and although he couldn't see any, Zack felt as though there must be walls to this tunnel. He had no control over his motion, yet he had no fear of hitting the sides. There was nothing to hold him, but strangely there was no sense of falling. He moved through the journey as driftwood is carried by a river, floating on the very force that propelled him forward, with no shore in sight. If it were not for the occasional flash of colored light zooming by, he couldn't even be sure he was moving. Then, as if waking suddenly from a particularly vivid dream, he found himself sitting on the bench.

He quickly raised his hand to block the unexpected flood of daylight and found that he was holding the finder, the green screw still in place. "Wow, nobody at school is going to believe this!" he said. The finder display still read:

Ready. Earth. Hold finder. Red to Return.

He was beginning to wonder if it ever said anything else. He stood and waved in the direction of home plate, figuring that Taylor would be looking, and gave a thumbs up sign to tell her that he was OK. He removed the green screw and put it in his pocket. He then pulled out the red one and spoke to it. "Well," he said, "I guess you're my ride home." He turned it in the hole until the threads grabbed hold. Almost instantly he found himself back in the darkness, unaware of the direction he was traveling but confident it would take him back. He was right, and a moment later, his twisted form poured out of the telescope eyepiece and solidified.

"Did you see me, did you see me?" Zack asked, jumping up and down. "Yes, and the red screw brought you back!" she replied. "Come on," he called, "I have to go call Jake and tell him about this, he'll be amazed." "I'm sure he will, but Zack, you can't tell anyone about this, at least not yet. We have to learn more about it first, where it came from and who it belongs to," she warned. "OK," he agreed, "but let's take it out again tonight, I think there's a full Moon."

Chapter Six

Click, Click, Print

L unch was one of their favorites, Peanut Butter Surprise. It was simply a peanut butter sandwich with the crust cut off and M&M chocolate candies hidden inside. They ate this so often that by now, the only surprise was not the chocolate, but how many M&M's they would find. However, the only mystery that Zack was thinking about was the telescope. As soon as he and Taylor had finished their food, they took their plates to the sink and headed for the computer in the family room.

Zack grabbed the mouse and double clicked on the Internet browser. The screen filled with a state map and the weather forecast. "Sunny with a high temperature of 81 degrees Fahrenheit today. Clear skies tonight with a low temperature of 65 degrees." Their father had set this as their "homepage" and they hadn't really given it much thought before, considering it just a page they had to get past before they could get to the instant messaging program or the online games. Now they realized it might actually have some purpose. "Clear skies tonight, with a low of 65," Zack announced in his best TV meteorologist's voice. "That means we should be able to *go to...*" he stopped, looked behind him cautiously and then continued, "I mean, *see* the Moon tonight."

Taylor tapped the screen, directing Zack to click on the box at the upper left corner of the monitor. It read, "Search the Web." He complied, clicking the white rectangle and moving the now flashing cursor inside it. Taylor typed "telescope" and hit the "enter" key. The screen changed almost immediately and listed the search engine's results. There were 10 paragraphs on the page, each with a title underlined and in blue. They both understood from a very early age that if the text was in color and underlined, it was probably a link to another web page.

Four of the links mentioned the Hubble Space Telescope, which Taylor knew from class was a school bus-sized telescope that took pictures from Earth orbit. It was above all the air and light pollution on the ground for a better view. Five other links were advertisements from stores selling telescopes and one said "Definition." "Click that one," she said. Zack moved the mouse until it was over the word "Definition" and clicked once. The page changed.

Telescope: An arrangement of lenses or mirrors or both that gathers light, allowing direct viewing, magnifying or photography of distant objects.

"Or travel to distant objects," Zack added with a smile. "Back," Taylor said, pointing to the browser's "Back" button. Zack clicked it and the search engine page reappeared.

"How many links did it find for 'telescope?'" she asked. "I don't know," Zack answered as he scrolled down. "There are 10 on this page and...oh," his heart sank as he read the words at the bottom of the page: "results 1-10 of 4,431,657." "This could take a while, huh?" he asked, knowing the answer. "I guess we need to narrow our search," Taylor offered. She typed "telescope travel," hit "enter" and the page was redrawn. "Results 1-10 of 407,000," they read. "We may as well start with the first one," Taylor accepted.

Together they spent the next 30 minutes reading the first few sentences describing each link. What they found was that most seemed to talk about a telescope that was small enough for a person to take with them on a trip. The web sites mentioned how lightweight the scopes were, how small or even how sturdy each was, but after reading through 7 pages of results, they realized what they knew from the start: there was no web site describing a telescope that could transport people to the place they were viewing. It was likely they had the only one. Who made it, who owned it and how it came to be buried in the sand were mysteries that would have to wait.

"If we can't find anything on where it came from," Zack suggested, "let's find out more about where it can take us." He typed "Moon" into the search engine and hit "enter." This time it returned nearly 22 million links, but fortunately the second one was called Moon Facts for Kids. He clicked and was rewarded with a simple web page that included a great photo of the Moon and a short list. It read:

The Moon is a satellite of Earth, orbiting around it.

The average distance to the Moon from Earth is 240,000 miles.

It takes almost 28 days for the Moon to make one complete orbit around the Earth.

It takes almost 28 days for the Moon to make one complete rotation (spin) on its axis.

The Moon is covered with craters made by meteor impacts.

The Moon is the only natural object in space that people have ever visited.

"We'll fix that," Zack declared. "What time does the Moon rise tonight?"

That evening the kids were back in the park, setting up the telescope as the last of the Sun sank below the western horizon. In the opposite side of the sky, the huge full Moon was already climbing. It had an orange glow caused by all the unseen dirt in the air and Taylor felt as though she could reach out and touch the giant ball. She aimed the telescope and saw the many craters that covered the surface. She knew from class that they had been created by impacts from meteorites over millions of years and with no wind or water to erode them, their circular marks would last millions more. She also noticed the dark flat areas called "Mare" or seas. She understood that this was just a name and that these were not bodies of water, but not wanting to have to convince Zack the area was dry, she decided to focus on a lighter area near the bottom of her view. It was a huge crater that seemed to have stripes leading away from its center in every direction.

"Take a look," she encouraged Zack. He closed one eye and put the other up to the eyepiece. "Whoa that's bright!" he exclaimed, pulling his eye back as though someone had just poked him with a finger. But it would take more than that to keep Zack away and he immediately stepped back into position. "Cool," he declared, "let's go!" He reached down into the plain metal box and came up with the two screws that controlled this unique device.

Taylor took the red screw and put it in her pocket, tapping the outside of her jeans once she had removed her hand as if to reassure herself that it was there. Zack held up the green screw between his right thumb and forefinger against the backdrop of the shining Moon for Taylor to see. She nodded her approval and he gently inserted the green screw into the finder's hole. Instantly the side of the smaller telescope turned to liquid and then solidified as a display screen. Both Taylor and Zack strained to see the new message as it scrolled across from right to left in red letters:

Ready. Earth's Moon. Tycho Crater. Hold Finder.

Red to Return.

"I've got butterflies in my stomach," Taylor said in an excited but slightly nervous tone. Zack wondered how anyone could really know what it felt like to have butterflies flying around in their stomach, but decided that this was not the time to ask. Instead, and with equal excitement in his voice, he simply said, "Let's go!" Taylor held Zack's left hand while he put his right on the finder. Slowly, cautiously Taylor moved her eye to the eyepiece.

Without warning, there was a rustling of branches in the tree behind them. Zack let go of the finder as they both spun around, straining to see and hear who could be approaching. The moonlight was bright, but only enough for them to see branches move as whoever it was moved closer. Neither of them moved, their feet frozen in place. "Hello?" Taylor called out. Her tone was uncertain as she wasn't sure if she wanted to be heard or not. There was no answer except the continued movement of the branches. "Is anyone there?" Zack tried. Then, low to ground, the dark masked face of a raccoon emerged from the bushes. Both Zack and Taylor's shoulders sank as they let out a sigh of relief; the raccoon, unconcerned with them, went about his task of finding dinner.

Now, with the butterflies gone from Taylor's stomach, they turned again to their travel plans. Once again, Zack placed one hand on the finder and the other in Taylor's hand. She moved her right eye to the eyepiece. For a moment she saw the magnificent crater Tyco, but almost immediately she began to feel slightly dizzy. Zack was feeling the same way as they both began to twist and spin into funnel clouds. The tip of Taylor's cloud was the first to be sucked into the eyepiece, and when nearly the entire vapor was gone, a small wisp that trailed and connected to Zack's cloud pulled him in also, until they were both gone. The raccoon hadn't noticed a thing.

Chapter Seven

One Giant Leap

Still holding hands, Taylor and Zack sped through the dark tunnel, floating side by side as if on some unseen magic carpet. "We're flying!" Taylor shouted in excitement. "EEE-Haw!" was Zack's reply. The apprehension that each had felt when they sailed through the tunnel alone the first time had now turned to exhilaration. They looked ahead in anticipation of their distant destination, but could see no sign of Earth's only natural satellite. Yet, after only a few seconds had passed, they found themselves out of the tunnel, stopped, in bright sunlight and in total silence.

It took a moment for their eyes to adjust to the sudden brightness. Instinctively looking down and away from the light, they noticed the ground beneath their feet looked gray and brown in spots, powdery and uneven. Zack thought it looked like some kind of strange desert sand, dry and barren, though he didn't expect to be seeing any camels. In the far distance, the ground rose to form a mountain range that encircled them. It was one solid wall sloping sharply up from the ground in every direction they looked. They had the feeling of being in the bottom of a very deep and wide bowl. A towering mountain stood in the middle of this valley. It stood alone, like a monument, with its wide base tapering to a knife-edged peak high above. Around it, the ground was mostly flat right up to the perimeter walls. There was so little there, yet there was so much to see.

They released each other's hand as they turned to look around in amazement. The sky was black, a perfect, solid, unwavering black. "I've never seen anything this black before," thought Taylor. Even the sky at the beach wasn't this dark, and yet they were standing in full sunlight! It was daytime on the Moon and the sky was darker than the darkest nighttime sky she had ever seen. The Sun was still there in a corner of the sky, but it didn't seem to light up the sky the way it did on Earth. It just appeared as a very bright ball surrounded by abrupt, total darkness. As from Earth, it was still too painful to look straight at it.

"Look at the stars," Zack whispered, tilting his head back as far as it would go. "The Sun is up and there are more stars than at night on Earth. How can that be?" A soft "beep, beep,

beep" reached his ears and as he looked to his hands for the source of the sound, he realized that he was still holding the finder. The screen said "Push for answer" with an image of a button. Zack looked at Taylor, shrugged his shoulders and pushed it.

They were two regular kids standing on the Moon, having just been instantly transported there by some strange telescope that they had been sucked into after digging it up on the beach. Taylor hardly thought that anything could amaze her more right then, but when a voice came out of the finder, she nearly fell over. The voice was calm, relaxed and sounded human, as opposed to a machine or computer. It was difficult to tell if it was male or female and it said:

"The atmosphere of Earth is like an ocean of air surrounding the planet. When sunlight (which is made up of all colors) hits it, most of the blue light is scattered, making the sky appear bright blue and making it nearly impossible to see stars in the daytime. They are still there, you just can't see them. The Moon has no atmosphere and so there is nothing to scatter the light and block the view of space and the stars."

Then the display changed to show:

Ready. Earth's Moon. Tycho Crater. Hold Finder.

Red to Return to Earth.

"No way, this is the coolest thing ever!" Zack declared. "It answered my question. You try," he encouraged. "OK," she said. "Where are we?" As before, the display offered the button. Zack pushed it.

"You are in the Tycho Crater on Earth's Moon. Named after Earth astronomer Tycho Brahe, this large impact crater is approximately 85 kilometers in diameter and 100 million years old and can be easily seen from Earth with binoculars or a small telescope."

"Or visited with a really cool one!" Zack gleefully added.

"OK," Taylor said, as she slowly lifted her right foot in the air and took a step. "That's one small step for a kid, one giant leap for kid-kind," she declared. "But no footprint," Zack pointed out. As she looked down at her feet, she realized that he was right. There was no mark in the powdery surface where she had placed her first step. In fact, there were no marks where either of their feet had been. It was as if they weren't touching the ground at all and yet they felt firmness under their feet. Zack began to stomp his feet, testing this strange development. He expected to see the fine gray dust kicked up, but when it didn't, he tried harder and began jumping. Zack leaped gently into the air, expecting to crash down, scattering sand. Instead, he kept going up! Taylor looked up as he floated up above her. "Wee!" Zack sang as he floated gently back down. "I'm as light as a feather." He jumped up again and bounded away from Taylor, pushing off each time his feet came in contact with the surface. He felt as though he was a balloon floating through the air, getting a tap every so often to keep him off the ground. "Wait," Taylor called after him. "Wait…for me!" This looked like fun and it seemed safe enough, so off she went, taking giants steps that seemed effortless. Each step equaled six steps back home. She was surprised at the amount of ground she was covering and caught up to Zack in no time.

Having only 1/6th the gravity of Earth on the Moon meant that everything weighed much less than it did normally. Zack, who weighed 54 lbs. on Earth, weighed only 9 lbs. on the Moon. "Bet you can't catch me," he challenged, kicking off again. "Just watch me," was the reply as she lunged for him, just missing. Taylor now weighed only 12 lbs. They giggled as they took turns being "it." Running was easy, but they found it surprisingly difficult to stop or change direction quickly. The result was a fair amount of falls and near collisions. In one instance, Zack dove for Taylor who merely jumped to the side and watched as Zack sailed by, falling to the ground and rolling several times before coming to a stop. They both laughed as they tried to catch their breath, Taylor bent over with her hands on her knees and Zack flat on his back.

Their panting was interrupted when Zack's arm shot out from his side, his hand pointing straight up. "Wow, look at that!" he exclaimed. Taylor straightened up and followed Zack's arm skyward. Her breath was just returning to normal following their game, but what she saw took it away again. In the inky blackness above them was a magnificent sight. There, hanging by itself, was a bright, beautiful Earth. The colors were somehow purer than they had ever seen. The blue was bluer, the white whiter, and the areas of green and brown richer than they could have imagined. A soft, curving blackness cut across the bottom of the planet, obscuring the lower third. Like the Moon as seen from Earth, the Earth had phases when seen from the Moon. Neither of them had expected this.

They both stared in silence as they examined the swirling colors, noticing how much more blue there was than green or brown. Taylor was sure the brown and green was land, but the white clouds covered enough of the view that she couldn't see the edges. This made it difficult for her to use the geography skills that had earned her an "A" in class just a few weeks ago. She turned her head at different angles hoping to recognize the funnel shape of South America or the "island" continent of Australia. It occurred to her that this ball in the sky was their home. For the first time, she wasn't thinking in terms of her street or town or even country. From here it all looked so small, so manageable, so easy to get from one place to another.

Only hours earlier it would have seemed almost impossible to travel from one side of the planet to the other and yet, there it was in one glance. She remembered Mr. Capella referring to it as "Spaceship Earth," but it wasn't until this moment that she truly understood what he meant. Their home was traveling through the vastness of space and everyone on it was a passenger riding in circles.

"Look, Moon angels!" Zack's words suddenly broke Taylor's concentration. She looked down at him still lying on the ground. He was moving his arms up and down along the ground as he had done after each of the last big snow storms. Zack couldn't tell from his point of view, but the ground where he was moving his arms was undisturbed. In fact, there were *no* markings where they had been running, jumping or falling. There was no disturbance in the ground at all! It was as if they hadn't been there. Taylor noticed this first, since she was standing. When she told Zack, he jumped up to see. The evidence, or lack of it, was clear, but just as he always had to push an already lit elevator button, Zack still had to test it further by trying to dig the toe of his shoe into the ground and kick up some of the fine gray powder. To the surprise of neither of them, nothing happened. He raised the finder and asked aloud: "Why can't we move the dirt?" The finder screen changed as before and Zack touched the button that now showed on the screen.

"Rule #1: Leave no trace."

This was the entire answer. "I wonder what that means!" he said to Taylor, his head tilted and left eye squinting as if trying to see the far off answer. "I think it means that there shouldn't be any sign that we were here after we leave. You know, pick up your trash, leave the place the way you found it so the next person can enjoy it. The stuff Dad is always talking about." "Oh, I get it," he nodded. "But it's not us cleaning up after ourselves. This thing won't *let* us make a mess," Zack pointed out. "Maybe taking responsibility for preserving the environment is really important where this telescope comes from. So important, they aren't leaving it up to us," Taylor said. "They must have seen my room," Zack suggested. "I meant to clean it up, really I did. Well, I'm just glad that they think breathing is a high priority, too. In case you haven't noticed, we're not wearing space suits. Even I know that there's no air to breath in space and astronauts have to bring their own oxygen along on any trip," Zack advised.

"I wonder what it's like where the telescope comes from," Taylor thought out loud. "I wonder if it's beautiful with big green trees and blue lakes and people who spend their days thinking up great inventions like this." "Or maybe they're giants with an eye on each side of their red heads, flying throughout the galaxy conquering other worlds," Zack countered. "Or maybe they're microscopic and live in a small puddle of acid on some distant planet and use telepathy to communicate," Zack continued. "Why don't we just ask?" Taylor suggested. "Yeah," Zack responded in a tone that said 'why didn't I think of that?' without actually saying it.

He reluctantly handed the finder to Taylor and she said, "Who are you?" The screen showed the usual information of where they were and how to get back. She asked again, this time a little louder on the chance it didn't hear her. The screen was unchanged. Once more she asked, this time starting with "Finder" in a commanding tone and following with her question, just in case it didn't know she was talking to it, but as before, the display remained steady. "Where are you from?" Zack called out. Still no change. "Who do you belong to?" Taylor questioned. An answer came immediately, but it was not coming from the finder. "It belongs to us!" Zack shouted, with a slightly frantic sound in his voice. "Finders keepers," he added as his proof. "You know that's not the way it works. This is too valuable. Mom and Dad will never let us keep it without trying to find the rightful owner first," she warned. "But we asked it who it belongs to and it wouldn't tell us," he pleaded. "Yeah right," she said in her most sarcastic tone, "I'm sure Dad will buy *that* explanation!"

At that moment, a small spot of brownish-gray dirt near Zack's right foot suddenly, but silently, exploded. A spray of the fine powder jumped up from the ground the way water splashes from a pool when a diver hits it. Most of the dirt fell back in a circular pattern around the newly formed hole, but the finer grains and dust continued up in every direction, as if trying to escape the impact that had just freed them from the surface. "Taylor, did you see that!" Zack excitedly asked. Moon dust now covered the tip of his right shoe. "How could I miss it?" she replied with equal surprise. "I thought nothing was supposed to change from our being here," he wondered. "That dirt definitely moved," Taylor confirmed. "But I didn't move it!" Zack pointed out. Two yards away another patch of ground exploded with the impact of an unseen speeding particle, then another behind them. "What's happening?" Zack cried. "I didn't touch anything, I promise."

These mini explosions were coming faster now and it was impossible to predict where they would hit next. Another burst of dirt erupted from between Taylor's feet. "Ah," she screamed, "run!" "Where?" asked Zack in frustration. "They're everywhere." "I don't know, just run," she commanded. They took off running through the open lunar desert with no shelter in site. As they ran, Taylor heard the beep of the finder. Her eyes went back and forth from the screen to the uneven ground in front of her. It was calmly answering Zack's question.

"The Moon is passing through a trail of dust and debris left behind when comet Swift-Tuttle last passed by here in 1992. Because of its orbit, the comet flies past here about every 130 years. The particles, most of which are the size of a grain of sand, are called meteoroids. If they burn up in Earth's atmosphere they're called meteors and when the bigger ones make it to the ground they are called meteorites. With no atmosphere on the Moon, the tiny ones are impacting the surface at high speed. You are experiencing a meteor shower. Take shelter."

Taylor shared the finder's comments with Zack as they ran, pausing after each sentence to take a breath. Puffs of powder were popping up all around them. When she finished, Zack, panting, said, "Do you mean to tell me that we're under attack from high speed dust?" "I'm afraid so," she said, "and we've got to find someplace to hide before we get hit. Follow me." Taylor turned without slowing and headed for the center of

44

the crater. It was the only place within site with rock formations taller than them. "We can hide underneath those rocks," she explained. "Only if we can get there," Zack replied as he struggled to keep up with her.

The shower was turning to a storm and multiple impacts were occurring everywhere they looked. They bounced along, half running, half floating and wishing for more speed. A large group of rocks stood in the distance, but neither of the kids was sure they could make it in time. One hit from this deadly dust could be fatal. The particles were so small and traveling at such high speed, they were invisible, and in the vacuum of space they were silent, too. Taylor realized that they had been lucky to dodge these mini-missiles so far, but there was no guarantee that their luck would hold out. They had to reach the shelter of those rock formations.

One of the larger pieces of debris, about the size of a grain of rice, crashed into the ground directly in front of Zack. "Whoa!" he called. He pushed off extra hard, as the clumps of dirt ejected from his path pelted his entire body just as his feet left the ground. This impact was larger than most, and the crater it created was a full six feet in diameter. Zack's leap just barely got him across, but his back foot caught the edge of the hole. "No!" he cried as his ankle twisted and he immediately knew that he was going to fall. His back foot flipped out from under him and his front foot quickly followed. His slow, twisting and graceful fall to the ground looked like a bad ballet move in slow motion. "Help!" he called. Taylor turned just in time to see him hit the ground and start to roll. "Zack!" she cried. In the back of her mind Taylor thought how odd it looked to have the moon soil bursting into the air all around them, but show no effect at all from Zack's fall and roll. She forced herself to stop, despite the inertia that tried to keep her moving forward. She took a few steps back and reached down her hand to help him up. "Come on," she pleaded, "we've got to get out of here." Zack struggled to his feet, regained his footing and they both resumed their sprint for the rocks. As Zack glanced back at the spot where he had just been lying, it exploded in a cloud of dust. "No more looking back," he told himself.

Finally, after crossing the seemingly endless remaining ground, they reached the first large formation of boulders. The huge gray and white rocks had sharp edges and were piled in a way that left a small, but mostly covered space under them. Taylor pushed off with one last step. "Dive for it!" she commanded as she ducked her head and glided into the safety of this natural fortress. Zack followed right behind her, dropping his right shoulder down and gently rolling on his back under the protective stone ceiling. Taylor grabbed and pulled him in just as a larger grain slammed into the ground at the "door" of their new shelter. A plume of soil filled the space, clouding their view and spraying them with the fine powder. "That was close!" Taylor said, catching her breath. "Let me get this straight," Zack began in his most sarcastic tone, "we can't leave a single mark that we've been here, but that comet can leave a trail of debris miles long that attacks us 130 years after it passed by! It's a crazy universe."

Taylor removed the green screw from the finder and put her hand in her pocket. "We better be getting back, Mom and Dad will start to wonder where we are," she explained.

When she took her hand out, she was holding the red screw. Zack looked up at her with big, sad eyes and extended his lower lip. Taylor knew what the look meant, but she put the red screw into the finder anyway and gave it a firm turn.

Chapter Eight

Blue

The Sun shined brightly the following morning, just as it had for each of the previous 4.5 billion years of its life. For Zack and Taylor, however, it may as well have been cloudy and raining, because that's how they both felt. It was the last day of their summer vacation and over a breakfast of orange juice, Reese's Pieces cereal with milk and Wonder Bread toast, they had told their parents about finding the telescope. They had only gotten as far as the part about bringing it home with them from the beach though, because both parents were frantically rushing around the kitchen going through their morning routines before they each left for work. It always seemed like they were late from the way they moved, gliding around the room at high speed in crisscrossing patterns like hockey players heading for different goals.

"That's quite a find!" their father exclaimed as he folded a piece of bread and took a bite, stuffing an apple into a brown paper bag. "That must be very expensive, I'm sure that the *owner* will be looking to get it back. Isn't that right, dear?" their mother asked. The three of them knew that the way she had said that it was more of an instruction than a question. "Yes, we know," Taylor moaned in understanding. "We're taking it to the police station lost and found after breakfast," Zack added with an equal lack of excitement. "Good, it's the right thing to do," their mother replied. "You never know," their father offered, "maybe no one will claim it and then you'll get to keep it." "Really, you think so?" Taylor perked up. "Now don't go getting their hopes up," their mother cautioned. "Valuable scientific equipment is bound to be missed," she said, putting on her coat.

Her words were softly spoken, but they were a crashing blow to the kids. Their father gave them a sad smile and shrugged his shoulders as he rolled his lunch bag closed and headed toward the door. "Taylor," her mother called, "you're babysitting your brother until we get home." "I'm not a baby," Zack corrected. "It's just an expression. Lunch is in the fridge. See you later, don't wander far, love you!" their mother said as the door to the garage closed behind her.

The bike ride to the police station was a wobbly one for Taylor since her handle bar basket, with the help of some string, held the long metal box. Zack followed close behind her on his flame painted BMX. Four blocks later, they were in front of the station. Both had passed it many times before, but neither of them had ever been inside. From the outside, it looked very much like any of the other low-rise office buildings in the area: a rectangular box with large smoked glass windows so that neither too much sunlight, nor curious eyes, could get in. On the way there, Zack had imagined metal bars on rows of cells filled with criminals caught red-handed. Now, for the first time, he was thinking about the phrase "red-handed," and why a criminal's hands would be red. "What could make them red? What could a criminal get on his hands to make them re-" He stopped. "Maybe I'll wait out here," he suggested taking a step backwards. "Not a chance," Taylor insisted, as she pulled his arm with her free hand.

Inside, it was surprisingly quiet. It looked more like a bank than anything else. There was a small carpeted lobby and a wall that came up half way to the ceiling. The rest of the wall was more of that dark smoky glass, but this glass had a gray metal circle in it that Zack knew was both a speaker and a microphone. Under it, there was a small opening in the glass through which you could pass things. As they walked side by side up to the window, a voice came through the speaker. "Can I help you kids? What ya got there, it looks awful heavy." The man's voice was strong, confident and friendly. "Uh, yes please,

50

I mean a box, uh, we found it," Taylor responded in a quiet, unsure voice. "Wait right there," said the speaker.

A moment later, they heard a metallic click as the lock on a door they hadn't even noticed before was released. The door opened and a tall man in a blue uniform came toward them. He had a gleaming silver badge pinned to his chest, and a gun belt with several other tools attached around his waist. His shoes were like mirrors and there was not a strand of hair on his head. "So," he said as he bent down to look Taylor in the eye. "Nice box, what's in it?" "A telescope," she said simply. "We found it in the sand at the beach and we don't know who it belongs to."

Zack just stared. His eyes went back and forth between the officer's bald head and his gun. "Alright then, let me see," the officer said as he took the box from Taylor's arms. Second thoughts about what they were doing flashed through her head, but she relaxed her grip. "My name is Officer Navi, what's your's?" Taylor told him their names. "Let's see if there's a name anywhere on this." He turned the box over and over looking for any identification or way to open it. Finding none, and too embarrassed to ask the kids how to open it, he said as he stood, "Well, no one has reported anything like this missing, so we'll hold it here in case they do." Zack was still staring. Taylor mustered her courage and asked, "If they don't, can we have it back?" "That's a possibility if no one claims it after 120 days," Navi replied.

Zack was silently doing the calculation in his head, then he blurted out, "4 months!" "Ah, your brother *can* talk," the officer announced as if making a discovery. "Trust me, it's never been a problem for him before," Taylor explained. "Yes, young man," said Officer Navi, "if the item is unclaimed after 4 months, we will call you and it will then belong to you. Why don't you give me your address and phone number?" Taylor did. "Thank you," the kids said in unison, turning to leave. "4 months!" Zack complained, "That's like forever." Normally, Taylor would have corrected him and told him he was exaggerating and that it wasn't really that long, but instead, she just walked straight ahead with her head down and said, "Yeah, I know."

Inside the police station, Officer Navi, still unable to find a way to open the box, wrote some information on a tag, attached it to the box and placed them both on the dusty top shelf of the last bookcase in the back row of the basement storage room. He turned off the light and locked the door.

Chapter Nine

Back to School

A couple of days had passed since Zack and his sister had turned the telescope over to the police, and he couldn't stop thinking about it. After 2 half days that started the school year, he was now sitting in his first full Integrated Reading and Language Arts class. "I.R.L.A," as it was known, was what his parents used to call "English." The class name had changed significantly since their time in school, but the first assignment of the new year was the same as it ever was. "Your assignment for today is to write a 1 page essay," the teacher announced, "entitled 'What I Did On My Summer Vacation.'" All of the students groaned at once, with the exception of Zack. "No problem," he said with a smile and started writing. He wrote non-stop, never looking up, for twenty minutes until the teacher told them to put their pencils down. By this time, he was already half way through his third page.

"Who would like to read for the class?" asked the teacher. Without hesitation, Zack's hand shot up. He strained to get it higher than anyone else's, as though the highest hand would somehow win. Seeing his eagerness, she selected him. Zack stood and walked proudly to the front of the room.

"My Summer Vacation," he read. "For my summer vacation I went to the beach and to the Moon." The class erupted in laughter, forcing him to stop reading. Zack looked up from the page uncomfortably. "Class, settle down now, settle down. Zack please continue," said the teacher. Zack's smile returned and he continued. Without mentioning the telescope or how he got there, he described jumping around on the Moon, chasing Taylor around in low gravity and his father snoring on the beach. The initial laughter died away as the class settled down and became captivated by his story. He described the view of Earth and how small and alone it looked.

When he finished his presentation, the room was silent. He stood alone at the front nervously waiting for the reaction. After what seemed like an eternity the teacher, sitting in the back of the room on top of another student's desk, broke the silence. "Well," she said, "it certainly sounds like you had an interesting summer. You didn't limit your story to one page, and I'm not so sure it's non-fiction, but your creativity was outstanding. I think you'll really enjoy our upcoming unit on creative writing. I'd say your essay merits an A-, congratulations. " Zack returned to his seat having enjoyed recounting his adventure with Taylor, but with a sadness that came from the uncertainty of not knowing if he would ever see the mysterious and wonderful telescope again.

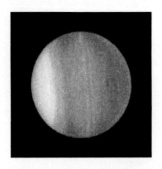

Chapter Ten

The Call

F our weeks had now passed since the kids had dropped off the telescope at the police station. Every day was another in which they wondered if *that* would be the day the first (as they thought of it) owner would appear to claim the amazing device and, perhaps, disappear into it, destined for home on the other side of the galaxy. Even though that would likely eliminate any chance of them getting it back, they still longed for something, anything to happen. The waiting was just too painful. Today, they would not be disappointed.

Though it would begin normally, today would be different for Officer Navi, too. It would be so amazing and unique, so unexpected, yet he would never even realize what had happened.

It was late morning and he was on duty at the front desk. That meant answering the phones, too, and he had already received calls about 2 minor traffic accidents, a man calling about a neighbor's ringing burglar alarm and one from a frantic mother who had locked her keys in her running car with her baby buckled into the back seat. In each case, he had calmed the caller, assured them that help was on the way, and dispatched one of the patrol officers to the scene. He then made a record of each caller in his logbook. It was a routine morning.

The next call he received was the one. It would be historic. It was what astronomers, scientists and science fiction fans around the world had been waiting for since people first began to wonder if we were alone in the Universe. Uncounted hours of lost sleep and millions of dollars were spent on special equipment, computers and huge satellite dishes, all devoted to searching for proof of the existence of other life in the Universe. All without success. Today, however, the answer would come in the ring of a simple telephone, and no one would notice.

"Police, can I help you?" Officer Navi said as he answered the phone. "Officer Navi," said a pleasant, friendly, but confident voice, "I believe you are holding something of mine." "Perhaps," the officer replied, a bit unsure if the voice was that of a man or a woman. "Why don't you describe the item to me," Navi suggested. "It is a metal box without handles or latches. There is no text on it, but it does have three symbols on one side and," the voice explained, "it contains a telescope."

"Give me your name please," requested Navi. "My name," the voice began, then paused. "My name is Pace, Mr. Sol Pace." "OK, Mr. Pace, we do have your item. You will need to come down to the station to pick it up," explained the police officer. "That is unnecessary," was the caller's even toned response. "This is a long distance call and I don't want the item returned," he added.

Navi's eyebrows jumped up in surprise and he glanced at the caller id display to see where the call was coming from. It was blank. "I want the children that found it to have it," Mr. Pace said. "Oh, well, that's very nice, but you'll need to come in and complete some forms," Officer Navi told him. "Impossible and unnecessary," was the reply. "You will give it to them in several months if I don't come to your station anyway, so you may give it to them now without me coming to your station. I give you my permission." Again the voice was calm and without emotion, but Navi could tell the caller's mind was made up. "Alright" he said, I'll see that they get the box." "Thank you," were the only further words from Mr. Pace. "Oh, Mr. Pace," Navi suddenly thought to ask, "how did you know that kids found the box?" But the dial tone had returned. Officer Navi put the phone back in its cradle. "And how did you know my name?" he asked the empty room, his voice trailing off. Officer Navi thought for a moment and then recorded the time and the caller's name in the logbook, content to leave the questions unanswered.

11:11 AM   Mr. S. Pace   Lost Property

Neither this police officer, nor any astronomer, scientist or science fiction fan, would ever know the magnitude of the brief conversation that had just occurred or how truly long distance the call really was.

Officer Navi opened his desk drawer and found Taylor and Zack's phone number and began to dial the local number.

Down in the dark and damp basement storage room, past the rows of stacked shelves of lost and found items and boxes of old paperwork piled 5 high, the plain metal box sat, untouched since it was placed there a month earlier. A small electrical charge briefly pulsed through the metal and the thick layer of dust that had accumulated, covering it, suddenly disappeared. The box was ready.

The message on the answering machine was waiting for them when they got home. It was short, but it had sent them both running (and cheering) for the door. Down at the police station, Taylor and Zack were afraid to ask too many questions about why they were being given the telescope three months earlier than they had expected, but they simply couldn't resist when they learned that the owner had called. Unfortunately, Officer Navi was unable to tell them much more than the caller's name, and the kids, not wanting to wait around on the chance that someone might change their mind, thanked him and quickly made their way home.

It was getting darker earlier now, and Taylor and Zack were anxious to get back outside with *their* new telescope. They knew without asking that they would have to finish dinner before their mother would allow them to go out, so Taylor had set the table a half hour early without being told, to speed the arrival of the evening meal. Homework had been completed, the telescope was by the door, and everything was ready, or so Zack thought, until Taylor whispered, "Where are we going tonight?"

For four weeks, Zack had daydreamed every day in class about the places they might go. In Art, he thought of traveling the solar system. In Math, he pictured himself spinning around the spiral arms of the Milky Way galaxy, and in IRLA, he flew between the stars, tracing the outline of the Big Dipper. But to actually go somewhere, they had to be able to see it with the telescope. The Moon had been easy enough to find, but what else was in tonight's sky? Stars were pretty obvious too, but which one was which?

"We need a map," Zack concluded. "Where are we going to get a map of the sky?" Taylor asked. "I don't think Dad has one in the glove compartment of the car." "Internet," was Zack's simple response as he turned and headed for the family room computer. He typed "night sky telescope map" into the search engine box and hit "enter." The screen changed almost immediately and displayed the results. The page said that it had found 335,000 matches, but they didn't need to look past the first one.

"That's what we want," he said, pointing the cursor at the top of the page and clicking. When the page refreshed, the words "Sky and Telescope" appeared as white letters in a red box at the top left corner of the new screen. "Interactive Sky Map" was written next to it with a rectangular box filling most of the page. The box had a black background with white dots scattered around. Thin purple lines connected some of the dots to form stick figure constellations. To the right, there was a place to enter a zip code and Zack entered the five digits at the end of their home address. Once again, the sky redrew itself, looking very similar to the way it had started, but with the white dots (the stars) moved slightly. This was the map of their sky at that moment.

Most of the dots were not labeled, but near the bottom left of the display sat an orange-yellow spot. Next to it was the word "Saturn." Taylor and Zack must have both seen it at the same time, because at the same moment, they both looked at each other with wide-eyed excitement and a big smile. Zack pushed back his chair, stood and extended his arm. His hand was flat with his palm to the ground. "Saturn?" he asked. Taylor instantly responded to the question by putting her own hand flat on top of his and declaring, "Saturn!"

Chapter Eleven

Close to Home

Dinner was Mom's turkey burgers and spaghetti. This was always a favorite, so she might have misunderstood the reason the kids had eaten so fast, finishing their entire meal before the chocolate powder had a chance to settle to the bottom of their poorly stirred chocolate milk. "We want to go outside, may we be excused?" Taylor politely asked. "Yes," their mother said, "but it's dark out and it's a school night," she continued, "put on a coat and don't stay out there too late. Papa will be here soon, he's staying through the weekend." "Yes, Mom" they both said. "And one more thing," she added, "I want you to keep that telescope in our backyard." "Uh, OK, we will," was the kids' reply as they moved toward the door. "I'd join you, but I have to do the bills tonight," said their father. "Maybe another time," Taylor offered.

While the kids put their coats on in the other room, their mother and father continued the conversation. "I'm so glad they found this telescope. They're so excited to use it and it will keep them close to home," she said. "Oh yes, I completely agree," he said.

Out in the backyard, the telescope was set up on a solid patch of ground. Taylor pushed on the tripod so that each of the three pointed legs sank slightly but firmly into the grass. They had printed the sky map from the computer and were now trying to match the star chart to the view from their backyard. Zack twisted and turned the page and held it over his head to better compare it to the sky above. They had turned off the back porch lights and as their eyes adjusted to the darkness, it became easier and easier to see.

They came to understand that the larger white dots on the star chart meant brighter, rather than bigger, stars and they soon found the matching pattern of stars from the chart in the grayish black sky above them. They looked low in the east for the orange dot. "I think that's Saturn," said Taylor as she pointed. It was just a small pale orange-yellow dot. It appeared very much like it was just another star but, like all planets, it didn't twinkle. "Point the telescope!" Zack anxiously commanded. He was so excited he was jumping in place. "Calm down," she advised, "I want to do this right."

Taylor gently lifted the large glass and metal tube from its protective case and raised it to the top of the tripod. She tightened the thumb screw that held it, but still allowed it to pan freely 360 degrees in a horizontal circle. Another part of the tripod head allowed the telescope to point up and down. Zack handed her the all-important finder scope, its outside currently shiny, smooth and solid except for the single opening that would hold a red or green screw. With the finder secured and riding piggy-back, Taylor pointed the telescope in the general direction of the pale orange point of light. She crouched down behind the tube and used it as a pointer, looking along the sleek exterior and drawing an imaginary straight line from her eye to her target. Next, she closed her left eye and peered through the finder with her right.

The dots didn't appear much larger since this finder, like most, had only modest magnification. Still, her target was in the field of view and she adjusted the telescope ever so slightly to the left to put the dot of her choice right in the center. Taylor moved her right eye to the main eyepiece. "Got it," she said. "Let me see, let me see," Zack sang, jumping again. "It's all fuzzy," Taylor half mumbled as she reached without looking for the focus knob. She found it and began to slowly turn it. "This should help bring it into…oooh, wow, it's beautiful!" Taylor softly exclaimed. "My turn," Zack loudly declared. He was now so excited he was getting maximum height in his jumps.

Taylor slowly and reluctantly pulled back from the telescope with her head being the last thing to move as though the rest of her body was leaving without her. It was as if the view would not let her go. Zack stepped up for his look. He could see the pale orange ball and rings tilted and shining brightly against the solid blackness. "It looks just like in books," he said, and it occurred to him to check the other end of the telescope on the chance that Taylor was playing a prank and had pasted a picture from an astronomy book there. "On second thought," he whispered "this is *not* like any book." It had a 3-D feeling that he had never seen before in any textbook or TV show. His voice was soft now, calm and muffled the way a person speaks upon entering a place of worship. The jumping had stopped and his eye was glued to the view.

Zack had no way of knowing it, but his and Taylor's reactions were frequently the same as for adults seeing the ringed planet for the first time. "It's real, it's really there," he thought.

He stepped backward, giving Taylor another opportunity. This time she was able to look more closely. She could see the shadow of the sphere on the back area of the rings, making them appear to disappear into blackness before they continued behind the planet itself. She asked Zack if he could see it and he took a turn at the eyepiece confirming Taylor's discovery. Then Zack made a discovery of his own. At first, the rings had seemed to be one solid white flat ring that surrounded the planet. Now, however, he was noticing that a thin black line split the ring into two flat rings circling Saturn. "Is that a black ring in among the white rings?" "Beep, beep, beep" was the quiet answer. Zack stood on his tip toes to read the response on the side of the finder.

"The largest black line in the rings is called the Cassini Division. It is a gap between rings A and B and is named after Italian-born astronomer Giovanni Domenico Cassini who discovered it in 1675. He made many other discoveries, including four of Saturn's moons."

"*Four* of Saturn's moons," Zack snapped "how many moons does it have?"

"Saturn has over 37 known moons. Titan is the largest. Titan is the 2ⁿᵈ largest moon in the solar system and is larger than the planets Mercury and Pluto. The only moon larger in the solar system is Jupiter's Ganymede."

"Cool, this is great!" Zack said. "But if it's bigger than some planets, how come Titan isn't a planet?' asked Taylor.

"Planets orbit the Sun, moons orbit planets. Titan orbits Saturn."

"Oh, I see," said Taylor. "And how many rings are there?"

"Saturn has at least six, labeled A-F, but more will be discovered. "B" is the largest."

"Thanks," she said, half expecting the finder to say, "You're welcome." "Wait," Zack interrupted, "You said *Saturn* has at least six, what else has rings?"

"All the gas giants have rings. That includes Jupiter, Uranus and Neptune. Saturn's are the brightest and easiest to see."

The view through the telescope was captivating and they could have easily spent an hour just taking turns. For a surprisingly long time, they had actually forgotten that they could do more than just look at the planet. Each time they took a turn viewing, the image seemed to show more detail. In truth, it wasn't the image that was changing, but the way they observed it. The more time they spent at the eyepiece, the better they were able to see. Without realizing it, they were "training their eyes."

The more detail they looked for, the more they were able to see. This was often the case for beginning astronomers. As a result, they were becoming better observers with each view through the eyepiece.

Nevertheless, as any baseball fan will admit, going to the game is better than watching it on television, and Zack and Taylor had the equivalent of seats in the dugout. This fact interrupted Zack's thoughts of how amazing the telescopic view was, causing him to break the hushed silence with the declaration, "Let's go!" Taylor abruptly looked up from the eyepiece as if hearing a strange sound. She looked from side to side and then said, "Why not?" She looked again to be sure that the telescope was aimed properly, filling the field of view with the planet and its rings. Zack was the keeper of the screws this time and he reached into his pocket and pulled them both out. Taylor took the green one from his open palm and watched him replace the red one in his jeans. They held hands. She inserted the screw in the finder while Zack squeezed his eyes shut in anticipation of the ride to come and then—nothing happened.

Zack opened one eye to see where they were. Taylor had both eyes open and was looking around. They hadn't moved an inch. "What happened?" Zack asked. As it had before, the soft beep of the finder made its way to their ears. They looked at it and to their surprise the finder was asking *them* a question:

"Saturn is one of the 'gas giants' of the solar system. It is a ball of tightly held gases with no solid surface. Unlike Earth or Mars, there is no place for you to stand. Would you like to go to Saturn's rings?"

As odd as it was for this amazing device to answer questions, it was something they could understand from their experience with their home computer. Having the machine ask *them* a question would take some getting used to. They looked at each other, a grin crossed Zack's lips as though he had just thought of something really fun to do that he knows full well he shouldn't be doing. "Sure," was their response. The finder display rippled and changed to:

Ready. Saturn's "B" Ring. Hold Finder.

Red to Return to Earth.

Again they clasped hands and Taylor bent to put her eye to the eyepiece. As she did, the suggestion of the finder echoed in Zack's mind. *"If we can't stand on Saturn because it's a ball of gas..."* he thought, *"how can we stand on the rings?!"*

Taylor's eye reached the eyepiece and the bright view of the 6th planet from the Sun came into focus. The now familiar

70

sensation began to swirl around them. It felt like a carousel ride at the county fair. To Taylor, the telescope and Zack didn't appear to move, but everything else was beginning to spin around them. Trees and grass became a blur of green, and houses a smear of white and black. The neighbor's porch lights spun into a circle of light. Within moments, they were speeding through the darkness. For their grandfather, watching this scene from his window in the first floor guest room of their house, it was the children that appeared to spin -- right into the eyepiece!

Chapter Twelve

Don't Look Down!

When they emerged from the tunnel (as they had come to call it), they were facing a bright light. It was bright, but not blinding, and it filled their view. It was like standing with your nose only a couple of inches from a wall, but they instinctively knew they were farther than that from the most beautiful planet in the solar system. The size of the planet, our system's second largest, was so overwhelming, it took a moment for them to realize that they were standing in space facing it. They knew it was round, but it was so immense that there was only a hint of curvature visible on either side. Taylor noticed that there were bands of pastel colors that wrapped the surface. Very pale pinks and yellows formed wide striped areas and there was a wispy cloudiness that seemed to cover the entire planet.

"Big, really big, really really big," was the phrase that kept repeating itself in Zack's head. He didn't realize it, but his mouth was hanging open again. Slowly, Zack's brain began to process what he was seeing and where he was. It was a little like looking out the window of a plane without the window, or the plane. His eyes followed the shining surface to the left -- Saturn, then space. To the right -- Saturn, then darkness. Up -- Saturn, then the pitch blackness of space. Down -- Saturn, then -- "Ahhhhhhhhh!" he screamed.

One of the common experiences we all share growing up on Earth is the idea that there is an up and a down to everything. This is not something that is necessarily taught, but it is something we understand from a very early age. Gravity is the reason. It's the kind of thing that is so basic to our everyday activities, like breathing, that we don't normally give it much thought. For Zack, this was *not* a normal moment and he was suddenly very aware of the concept of up and down and the need to have something under him to prevent the effects of gravity from causing him to fall. The concern he had about having a place to stand was terrifyingly real.

Fortunately, two things saved him. First, he came to understand that, remarkably, he seemed safe and was not falling. In space, the force of gravity is so small compared to what's on Earth that it appears to be non-existent. That's why things "float." Second, he was standing on a chunk of ice, no bigger than his feet, floating in space. The fact that there was nothing solid "under" the ice itself didn't seem to bother him. In space, there is no up or down and without that, a person cannot fall. In fact, he could float in space just as easily as the ice. He chose not to focus on this, and once he realized that he had something to stand on, that he wasn't in danger of falling, he began to look for Taylor. He found her about 20 feet away on her own chunk of ice.

As they began to examine their surroundings, they saw the giant ball of Saturn in front of them. Between them and the planet was a group of ice chunks. The chunks extended out to their left and right as far as they could see. Behind them was open space and then, in the distance, more blocks of ice and rock. "Where are the rings?" Taylor asked aloud. "Beep, beep, beep" called the finder, reminding her it was in her hand. Taylor examined the display and read it out loud for Zack's benefit. "It says, 'Saturn's rings are made up of a collection of chunks of ice, rock and dust particles that are held in place around the planet by its gravity and the gravity of Saturn's many moons. At least one moon has been observed to cause waves in a ring as it orbits nearby. You are at the edge of the Cassini Division and the "B" ring.'" "What?" Zack questioned. "These *are* the rings," Taylor concluded, "we're standing on them!" "Wow" he exclaimed, "I thought the rings were solid, like a race track."

The chunks floated silently around them, appearing motionless. They looked to Taylor like rocks sticking up above the surface of a pond, like a path to tip-toe across. She gingerly stepped to the nearest stone, extending her arms unnecessarily out to her sides for balance. She made it easily and decided to keep going. She stepped to the next one more confidently. "Come on," she called to Zack, and he took a step nearer to her.

Taylor's confidence was building with every movement. She pretended to throw something down on one of the rocks ahead, then she hopped forward with both feet at once, her left and right feet each landing on their own rock at the same time. She continued forward with her right foot hitting a single mass of ice, her left bent up behind her. She then bent over, pretended to pick up the imaginary marker and hop on, finishing with both feet on separate rocks. "Come on, you try" she suggested. "Me? Hopscotch? No way!" was Zack's predictable response. "OK then, suit yourself," Taylor countered, as she turned and jumped forward.

Taylor began to pick up speed as she continued along the unique path of stepping stones, hopping from one to the next. Zack noticed Taylor pulling away from him and, like most little brothers, interpreted it as a challenge. Zack yelled, "Go!" and took off leaping from ice boulder to ice boulder. Taylor looked over her shoulder at the sound of his shout and adjusted her pace.

Like most big sisters, she was not about to let her little brother get the best of her. The race was on. They hopped around the "B" ring, from ice block to ice block. Taylor felt like she was in a slow-motion ballet as she floated along. Zack was gaining on her. It was the solar system's first running race and the track was Saturn's rings. "I'll race you to that big one up there, "Zack challenged as he drew even with Taylor. "You're on!" she panted, stretching to regain her lead. Her legs were longer, but he was a faster runner. Zack edged ahead, but Taylor pointed her toes and kept pace with him. Her three years of ballet classes were coming in handy in a way no one had ever expected. They reached the finish line rock, touching it at the same moment. "Tie," they both called out. Zack grabbed the cold hunk and held on, but Taylor's fingers couldn't hold the slippery surface and she kept on going. "Hey, where are you going?" called Zack.

Taylor, who was concentrating more on winning than stopping, realized too late that with the reduced gravity of space and lack of friction, she would have to stop herself or she would simply keep going. "Zaaaaaack" she cried out, waving her arms and feet. "Grab on to something," he frantically instructed. "I'm trying," she cried, her hands slipping off the frozen rocks as she coasted past them.

She was traveling feet first now and watched the helpless expression on Zack's face as the image of him became smaller and smaller as she drifted slowly away. She was moving away from the concentration of rocks, dust and ice that formed the "B" ring and further into the gap between it and the "A" ring, the Cassini Division. It was very quiet now, and Zack's calling of her name had faded with the distance. He was waving his arms, crossing them back and forth above his head as if signaling a rescue plane, but none was coming. The magnificent view of the planet's shining belts of pale pink and yellow no longer drew her attention, nor did they have their earlier calming effect. Instead, she would have to calm herself and focus on a way to get back to Zack and avoid becoming the newest satellite of this beautiful world. She had no desire to become the first person to orbit another planet with or without a spacecraft.

Her thoughts turned back to Zack himself. At least he was safe, or was he? Stranded on a chunk of ice in one of Saturn's rings with no way home wasn't much better than her current fate. "He can't get back to Earth because I have the finder," she thought as she squeezed the cold metal tube in her hand to confirm that she still had it. "I have the finder," she repeated. An idea suddenly came to her. "I can use it to get back to Earth, then come back for Zack!" Taylor's heart rose with the thought. She looked down at the display. It read:

Ready. Saturn's Rings, Cassini Division, Red to Return.

"Red to return," she read. "Red to return." Her brain made a connection and it hit her hard. Zack had the red screw. Without it, she couldn't get back and without the finder he couldn't get back either. They were both stranded, separately. Her heart sank. That couldn't be it; she didn't want to believe it.

"There must be another way," she thought. The finder and telescope had taken them to the Moon and back safely, she reasoned. It had protected them from the 231 degree Fahrenheit temperature of the Sun on the Moon's surface and the -315 degree Fahrenheit temperature in the shade. It had transported them over 37 million miles to Saturn's rings after preventing them from trying to land on the planet's gaseous surface. It had even enabled them to speak to each other when, without air or a radio, there was no way for the sound of their voices to travel. Taylor couldn't believe that it would abandon them now. The telescope obviously came from a much more advanced society and the finder, or at least its makers, knew a lot more than she did, they had to.

That was when it struck her. She didn't need to figure out the answer. All she had to do was ask the finder. Still floating backwards, and ¼ of the way through her first orbit, she raised the finder, bringing the display into view. She was rapidly approaching the line between day and night on the planet. It was known to astronomers as "The Terminator." Of course, Taylor didn't know that, but she did know that if she didn't do something very soon, she would drift into darkness around the dark side of the planet. Using the fingertips of both hands to securely hold it and still leave the display visible, she asked the most important question she had ever asked anyone (or anything). She spoke slowly and clearly to prevent any misunderstanding or need to repeat herself. "How can I get back to Zack?" The finder display rippled like raindrops in a puddle. The display settled almost immediately and the words appeared. "Of course," Taylor sighed. "I should have guessed."

It was simple, but she was running out of time. She would need to act fast. By this time, Zack was so far away that he appeared to Taylor as just another dot. It was impossible for her to pick him out from among the other dots hanging in space that made up the "B" ring. She knew he had to be close to the horizon by now and hoped that he had not yet set below it. With the strong possibility of Zack disappearing behind the limb of Saturn, and the terminator line of darkness approaching from behind her, she raised the finder once more to her eye and scanned the field of view.

The finder did not have anywhere near the magnification of the larger telescope, but it was enough for her to tell the difference between a block of ice or rock and her brother (he had hair). She knew he wouldn't have moved far from the miniature island he was clinging to as she slewed the finder back and forth in a sweeping motion. The darkness was nearly upon her. If she entered it, she would almost certainly miss her chance to spot Zack and would have to complete another orbit. Since she knew that this was the second largest planet in the solar system, she was desperate to avoid this.

Suddenly she stopped her scan. "Is that him?" she asked herself at the sight of a human shaped object. "No, just a rock," she muttered in answer to her own question. She continued her desperate search. Another oddly shaped chunk of ice, but still no luck, and then another. "There are so many!" she complained to the vastness of space. "Relax Taylor," she told herself. "Keep at it, you'll find -- there he is!" Zack was sitting cross-legged on top of a medium sized ice ball calmly looking around. He appeared to be pretending it was a magic carpet and showed none of the worry that had filled Taylor. He had his arms extended, one pointing up and the other down, like a plane's wings banked in a turn. From her silent view through the finder, Taylor could see that her brother had his mouth open, apparently making engine noises completely unaware of, or uninterested in, the fact that wings are useless in space without air on which to ride.

The darkness was now upon Taylor and Zack was disappearing below her horizon. She fought to hold Zack in the field of view using her left hand as she reached for the green screw with her right. The edge of Zack's rock was now "touching" the limb of the planet. There were only seconds left. She would have only one chance. Steady on her target, she gently turned the green screw. An instant later, she was standing in front of her brother who was still seated cross-legged and just completing his imaginary turn. "Could you move please?" Zack asked, gesturing for Taylor to move to one side while tilting his head to see around her. "Zack, it worked! You're safe, too!" Taylor gushed, bending to hug him. "Well yeah," Zack responded, confused over what the big deal was. "Could you -- move please?" he added. Taylor shifted out of his way. He continued his imagined magic carpet ride. "What are you doing?" Taylor finally asked, slightly annoyed that he didn't seem concerned. "Playing," was his simple response. "Playing?" she exclaimed. "Yeah, I'm imagining that I'm flying around Saturn and I'm following the rings as my route." "Imagining?" Taylor questioned. "Zack!" she called, demanding his attention, "you *are* flying around Saturn!" "I know," he calmly replied, completely missing her point. "Hey, how was your trip?" he asked, as though just realizing she had returned.

Chapter Thirteen

Red Handed

Their grandfather was the kindest man they had ever known. They had called him Papa ever since they could talk because, as a toddler, Taylor couldn't pronounce Grandfather or Grandpa, and the name stuck. He had a warm smile, an easygoing nature, and a hug whenever he came to visit. He never arrived empty handed, either. His gifts, while not extravagant, always seemed to be exactly what they wanted, proving that it *is* the thought that counts. He was a proud and private man and though he couldn't get around as easily as he used to, he had been known to get down on the floor to play with his grandchildren without worrying about how he would be able to get back up.

He could also keep a secret, a fact that would be critically important to the kids, because as they emerged from the telescope back in their yard, their forms solidifying next to it, they found him standing there with his arms crossed and eyes wide in amazement. They stood in complete silence for what seemed an eternity. "Hi Papa," they each finally and weakly said in turn. The look on their faces was the same one they usually had just before getting a shot at the doctor's office. It was the look that said, "I know that pain is coming and there's nothing I can do about it." Papa grabbed one of them in each arm and pulled them in for a tight hug. "Why don't you pack up this wonderful telescope of your's and come inside for some hot chocolate," he suggested.

The kids, each with a cheek pressed against his chest, shot a glance of confused surprise at each other. They were sure that there was no possible way he hadn't seen them emerge from the eyepiece as a swirling cloud of smoke and solidify into his two grandchildren. It was dark, but even a grown-up couldn't have missed that.

Inside the kitchen, papers were strewn across the table. Their father sat with his checkbook, a calculator and a nearly empty mug of coffee. As they entered the room, he looked up and said, "So, how was it? Wait, don't tell me, let me guess," he offered. "It was out of this world." He smiled and waited for the usual reaction to his bad jokes. "Da-ad," they sang in unison. Papa just smiled, remembering when his son, their father, reacted in exactly the same way to his jokes so many years ago.

"How about that hot chocolate?" Papa suggested. "Oh, I'll get it," offered their mother as she took three mugs down from the cabinet. "Wait right here," Papa instructed. He disappeared from the room, but returned a moment later with two gift wrapped items. One was flat and square, the other was small and rectangular. "This is for you," he said to the kids as he handed each one a gift. "I think you'll want to share these," he added.

Both were covered with the same wrapping that featured little yellow stars against a dark blue background, but this was barely noticed as the kids tore into the paper, casting it aside and adding to the pile on the table. "It's a flashlight," Zack announced as he switched it on. "True," Papa agreed, "but not the usual kind." Zack immediately learned what he meant. "Hey, it's red!" "Yes, that's to preserve your 'night vision,' it helps keep your eyes adjusted to the darkness and makes it easier to see." "Oh, I *see*," joked Zack. Taylor and her mom shared a look. "It seems the bad jokes are hereditary, passed down from father to son," Mom concluded. "That's my boy!" Dad said with a proud smile.

All eyes now turned to Taylor as she examined her gift. It was a thick cardboard wheel under a colorful cardboard cover. The cover had a large oval opening in it that allowed a portion of the wheel underneath to be seen, with the letters N, E, S, and W printed on the four sides along with the months of the year. The wheel showed stars and constellations through the opening. Taylor looked up with a puzzled expression on her face. Papa read the question on her face and answered, "It's a planisphere, a kind of sky map. Just turn the wheel until the time of day printed here matches the month we're in. The constellations you see through the cardboard window are the ones in our sky now." Taylor's expression turned from puzzlement to understanding and a smile crossed her lips. "Thanks," she said and Zack quickly agreed, "Thanks Papa." Taylor looked back down at the planisphere and froze. "Wait," she said, "how did you know?" A wave of concern rolled over her. What did he know about their adventures before he arrived tonight?

Before he answered, she realized that this might not be the best time to find out, mom and dad being in the room. But he said, "Your father told me about the new telescope and how much you were enjoying it. I thought some accessories might be helpful." He winked at her. "Great- uh, thanks!" "You're very welcome," he replied with a smile. "Great things, those telescopes," their father declared, "fun and educational, and with a little imagination they can take you to far off places." "You have no idea," the kids quietly replied, smiling to themselves.

Chapter Photo Puzzle

The clues below refer to the photos at the start of each chapter.

ACROSS

1   Chapter Thirteen – A dirty snowball.

5   Chapter Nine – Do you really need a clue for this one?

7   Chapter One – Really bright.

9   Chapter Six – The rover Opportunity's new home.

11   Chapter Three – Wrongly called the evening "star."

12   Chapter Seven – Won't hold up your pants.

13   Chapter Eight – Home of the Great Red Spot.

DOWN

B